THE SEARING MYSTERIES

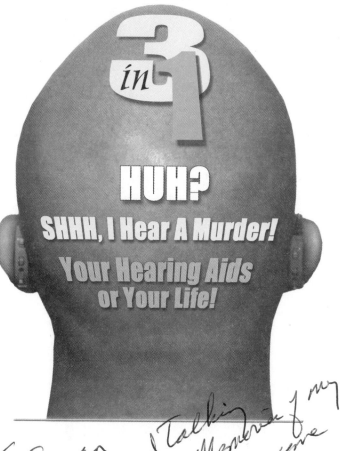

3 in 1

HUH?

SHHH, I Hear A Murder!

Your Hearing Aids or Your Life!

To Susan,
I so enjoyed talking of my
with Mary Ellen. Memories
Time in Berrien Springs came
rushing back. I hope you like
these stories.
Fondly,
Rich

Richard L. Baldwin

OTHER BOOKS
by Richard L. Baldwin

Fiction/Mystery

The Louis Searing and Margaret McMillan Mystery Series
>   A Lesson Plan for Murder
>
>   The Principal Cause of Death
>
>   Administration Can Be Murder
>
>   Buried Secrets of Bois Blanc: Murder in the
>   Straits of Mackinac

Fiction/Spiritual

>   Unity and the Children

Non-Fiction

>   A Story to Tell: The History of Special Education in
>   Michigan's Upper Peninsula (1892-1975)
>
>   The Piano Recital

Contribution Policy of Buttonwood Press

A portion of each book sold is contributed to Self Help for Hard of Hearing People (SHHH), 7910 Woodmont Avenue, Suite 1200, Bethesda, Maryland 20814. Website: http://www.shhh.org

Self Help for Hard of Hearing People is a volunteer, international association of hard of hearing people, their relatives and friends. It is a nonprofit, non-sectarian educational organization devoted to the welfare and interests of those who cannot hear well.

Dedication

This book is dedicated to all persons with hearing loss, all who love us, all who advocate for us, and to all who tolerate our idiosyncracies.

Published by

BUTTONWOOD PRESS
P.O. Box 716
Haslett, Michigan 48840

Printed in the United States of America

Baldwin, Richard L.
    The Searing mysteries / by Richard L. Baldwin. -- 1st ed.
    p. cm.
    CONTENTS: Huh? -- Shhh, I hear a murder -- Your hearing aids or your life!.
    SUMMARY: Private investigator Louis Searing is the lead detective in three short stories involving persons with hearing loss and the SHHH organization--Self Help for Hard of Hearing people. Two of the three cases are murder mysteries, the third a failed bank robbery.
    Audience: Ages 12 and up.
    ISBN 0-9660685-6-4
    1. Searing, Louis (Fictitious character)--Fiction.
2. Michigan--Fiction. 3. St. Paul (Minn.)--Fiction.
4. Detective and mysery stories.   I. Title.

PS3552.A451525S3 2001   813'.54
                       QB121-108

Acknowledgments

I wish to thank several people who helped make this book of short stories possible. First I thank my wife Patty Moylan Baldwin for years of compassion and understanding of my imperfect hearing and the personality that goes with it. Patty gave me advice and suggestions for telling these stories.

I thank the people of Buttonwood Press whose dedication to a good book is appreciated. I thank my editor, Gail Garber; my proof reader, Joyce Wagner; and my typesetter/cover designer, Marilyn "Sam" Nesbitt for their talents, skills, and timely attention to a rather tight production schedule.

I am indebted to Mr. Christopher Olson of East Lansing, Michigan, whose head is prominently displayed on the cover of this book.

In 2000, I attended the Self Help for Hard of Hearing People (SHHH) convention in St. Paul, Minnesota, and presented a session on writing fiction. I asked for suggestions from the audience for the story, Your Hearing Aids or Your Life. The following offered an idea which I included in the story. Thanks to Penny Allen of Port Orchard, Washington; Michael Bower of Auburn, Washington; Harriet Frankel of Atlanta, Georgia; Ken Goodmiller of Fincastle, Virginia; Linda Lundeen Moen of St. Paul, Minnesota; Mark Rosing of Cincinnati, Ohio; Nancy Wright of Jerome, Michigan, and Pat Vincent of Grove City, Ohio. I also wish to thank Pat Nelson of Hudson, Wisconsin, who provided me with a transcript of my session in St. Paul.

There were a number of people who offered a thought or suggestion to the stories. Thank you to Hal Bate, Ron Fenger, Gary Geisen, and Ann Liming.

HUH?

THE SEARING MYSTERIES

Setting: Bark River, Michigan
10 a.m. E.S.T.

The thief, wearing a bandanna over his nose and mouth, looked into the eyes of a Bark River Savings and Loan Bank teller and said, "Give me all your money and nobody will get hurt."

"Huh?" Lenore Coscarelli, the young and vivacious teller replied.

"What's this 'huh' stuff? I'm robbin' your bank. Give me all your money and nobody will get hurt," he said, with considerably more volume.

Lenore had a significant hearing loss. Given the muffled voice and the absence of visual clues, she had trouble understanding what he said.

"Can't hear you! Something about a monkey and getting Bert?" Lenore replied.

"Listen, you deaf or somethin'?" bellowed the impatient thief. "Give me the cash!"

"Where's the bash? Am I invited?" Lenore said with a smile while flicking her eyelashes at the bold thief.

"Don't get smart with me!" the thief replied, brandishing a gun and pointing it at Lenore. "Do you understand this?" he asked, waving the small pistol. "Now, give me your money!"

"Don't say I'm a dish and don't call me honey! How do you want the bills? Fifties? Hundreds? Tens? Fives? Ones?" Lenore asked, her heart pounding in her chest.

"All of it!"

"Fit? Fit in what? You got a sack for this cash?" Lenore asked.

"You got a bag, stuff it in your bag!" the thief demanded angrily.

"Don't tell me to stuff it, and don't call me a hag! Show a little respect, or you're not getting anything!" Lenore snapped back.

By now, the other tellers had had enough time to see a problem and to activate the silent alarm. One of the tellers had slipped away to inform the bank president, Dick Ely, who immediately put emergency procedures in place.

The thief knew he had little time to get out of the bank and into the getaway car. He took the bag although it contained only a few bills as Lenore had done such a marvelous job of stalling the thief and giving him practically nothing.

The thief ran from the bank as the Bark River Police were approaching. The police chased him, but he got away weaving in and out of alleys and down narrow streets.

The bank had recently purchased an audio system to record and monitor teller-client interactions. The tapes were kept for twenty-four hours and then erased and reused.

The police immediately took possession of the taped interaction between Lenore and the robber.

Lou Searing, hard-of-hearing and wearing two behind-the-ear hearing aids, arrived on the scene. He talked to Dick Ely, the president of the bank who sported a full moustache. Lou couldn't quite understand what he said when, like Lenore, he was denied visual clues.

"The thief got away with a bag of cash," Dick said exasperated.

"The guy had a rag and a rash?" Lou asked.

"No, he took a bag of CASH."

"Oh, sorry, I hear ya," Lou replied.

"Between you and Lenore, I can't seem to get my thoughts understood," Dick replied, a bit frustrated.

"Yeah, it's as stressful for us as it is for you. We need to be patient with each other. We'll get this solved."

Lou and Lenore had little trouble communicating with each other. Both gleaned information from lipreading and amplified sound. Lou was eager to get a description.

"What did the thief look like?" Lou asked.

"He was wearing a Harley-Davidson bandanna for a mask," Lenore replied.

"Well, that's a start. Can you describe him a bit more?" Lou asked.

"He was about six feet tall with a full head of brown hair. He wore jeans, a black T-shirt, and the bandanna I already told you about."

"He had a banana?" Lou asked with a puzzled look on his face.

"No, not a banana, a bandanna. You know, a handker-chief."

"Oh, yeah, a bandanna," Lou said with a chuckle. "Did you notice anything about his hands? Did he wear rings, a watch, have any markings on his hands?"

"Can't help you there, Lou. I was looking at him and trying to figure out what he was saying. It was obvious he was there to rob us. You don't come up to a teller's window wearing a mask to draw out a couple of twenties."

"No, I imagine not," Lou said with a chuckle. "OK, typical guy with a Harley bandanna?"

"That's all I can do for you, Lou."

"I'll take it, my friend," Lou said, jotting down the information on his notepad.

Lou talked with the police detective on the scene, Detective Sergeant Ann Liming. Ann didn't appreciate Lou being involved. She thought she could easily solve this case. And, since it was a bank robbery, the FBI would be involved as well. But Ann respected Lou and knew he could be trusted to cooperate.

Lou knew that the Harley bandanna wasn't a lot of help. Harley-Davidson items were very popular and accessories were common. Lou had a couple of T-shirts of his own and a few other items as friends and family knew his fondness for motorcycles. The physical description was minimal and they didn't have a photo to take to Harley dealers for possible identification. Lou quickly learned from the police that past bank robberies didn't have any similar suspects. To be honest, Harley-Davidson riders have more of a reputation for giving money to fundraisers and to helping people than ripping off a bank.

The guy must have been pretty desperate to think he could rob a bank, thought Lou. People who are Harley-Davidson aficionados usually congregate. They go to rallies like the big ones in Sturgis, North Dakota; Daytona, Florida; and Milwaukee, Wisconsin, the home of the Harley-Davidson corporate headquarters. There were tens of other smaller gatherings.

Lou knew that a "Bless the Bikes" rally would be taking place in Escanaba, Michigan, in a couple of days. It just might be that the robber could use a little forgiveness along with a blessing for his Harley. The rally would be on Sunday so Lou made arrangements to attend. He contacted the priest, Father David Dubay, who was also a biker. His nickname was "Father Speed."

"Could I ask for your help, Father Dave?"

"Sure, Lou. It must have something to do with a crime of some sort?"

"Bank robbery. The FBI and the Bark River Police are conducting the investigation. I got a call from my Self Help for Hard of Hearing People (SHHH) friend, Lenore Coscarelli, a teller at the bank. She suggested I come over and see if I could help. I didn't want to let a good friend down, so I hustled over."

"What can a biker priest do to help a detective looking for a bank robber?"

"Well, I think the thief may have some connection to Harley-Davidsons."

"Let's not get into stereotypes, Lou. You know that bikers are mostly compassionate people and law-abiding citizens."

"Oh, I know. But, the thief used a Harley-Davidson bandanna for a face mask and I'm thinking that people with Harley accessories like to congregate. I know your 'Bless the Bikes' rally is coming up Sunday afternoon in Escanaba."

"Hundreds of Harley riders and owners of other makes as well will be on hand. The weather looks like it will cooperate. But, I still don't see where I come in."

"I was thinking if you offered a confessional experience for the bikers, the thief might confess to stealing the money."

"Oh, Lou. You know that anything shared in a confessional is private. I couldn't divulge anything I heard."

"I know that, but I thought you could tip me off if somebody confessed to the robbery."

"Sorry, not a chance. I'm sorry about the theft, but what I hear doesn't go anywhere, ever."

"I understand. Guess it was a ridiculous request. I'll be at the rally and maybe I'll see you there."

"Bringing your bike, Lou?"

"Not this time, Father. If you don't mind, my '87 Sportster would appreciate your blessing in absentia."

"I'll make sure your Sportster's included."

The "Bless the Bikes" rally in Escanaba was attended by hundreds of motorcyclists and their beautiful machines. They congregated in a large pasture west of town. It looked like a massive class reunion as people recognized one another, looked at each other's bike, and shared a cold drink, a laugh, or the latest information about Harleys.

Lou was dressed in his Harley-Davidson cap, a Harley-Davidson T-shirt from Juneau, Alaska, jeans, and boots. He carried a clipboard with a hidden microphone in it. He looked like a biker who was taking a survey which is what he was doing, or pretending to do. He walked all over the field looking for anyone with a full head of hair, a Harley-Davidson bandanna and standing about 6 feet tall.

What Lou found was a whole set of biker communities. He saw a group of people with "SHHH Members Love Their Harleys" T-shirts. SHHH is the acronym for the organization, Self-Help for Hard of Hearing People. He wandered over and began to talk to one of the women, Lee Yerrick, who was in full biking regalia. She said that they were from the Lansing, Michigan area. They always made an effort to come to this rally.

Their goal was to raise money for their chapter by collecting donations in shopping centers or restaurants along their way to Escanaba. Kay Hare, one of the members, is a magician who specializes in card tricks. Another, Ruth Carpenter, plays the harmonica and gets folks dancing to her songs. A third, Jo Ann Russell is a marvelous singer of country songs. Lillie Mae Parker and her sister Willie Beard tell jokes that make everyone laugh and wonder why the sisters are not on television. Lou told Lee that he was a member of SHHH and could use a little help.

Lou asked the Lansing SHHH folks to go on a scavenger hunt of sorts: "I'm looking for a guy about 6 feet tall, full head of hair and wearing a Harley-Davidson bandanna. Can you folks try and find a guy that meets that description?"

The Capital Area Chapter agreed to comb the area and meet back in a half-hour to report if any potential six footers with bandannas were sighted. Thirty minutes later, they reconvened and tallied their results. They had seen five guys who met the description. Lou decided to try to find each one.

Lou thought it best to use a "taking a survey" technique to see if he could pull out any other clues. The first guy, Peter, seemed too tall and too big but he went through his questions: "How long did you bike to get here? More or less than 50 miles? Is this your first rally? How did you hear about it? Will you come back? How many people did you come here with? What kind of bike do you have? Then he asked Peter for his name and address saying he'd probably get a thank you note from the marketing professor at the university. Peter answered all questions and willingly wrote down his name and address.

The second person Lou interviewed was in direct contrast to the first guy in that Lou thought he was too short to be a suspect. But, he asked his questions, got his answers and obtained a name and address.

The third guy wore a dark bandanna that had the Harley-Davidson company logo on it, and he had a look about him that Lou thought made him a suspect. "Excuse me. I'm taking a survey of Harley owners and I'm hoping you'll answer a few questions for me."

"What's in it for me?"

"Nothing. I'm getting answers from a random group of riders for a marketing firm who wants to help other rally organizers. You might help some people put on another one of these rallies, but other than that, I guess nothin's in it for you."

"What kinda questions you askin'?"

"Got about ten of 'em here. Nothing personal."

"Ask and if I don't like the question, I'll shut up. That okay with you?"

"That's fine. The first question is, how far did you ride to get here? Less than 50 miles or more than 50 miles?"

"I'm thinking it was more."

"Stinkin' and sore? Is that what you said, you're sore from the ride," Lou said a bit confused.

"I said, MORE. You deaf or somethin'?"

"Not really deaf. I've got a hearing loss and wear a couple of aids. Sometimes I misunderstand, like then. Sorry."

The guy shook his head and said, "Next question? Let's get a move on. I've got things to do."

"Sing the blues? Is that what you said?" Lou asked

realizing it was totally out of context but that's what he thought he heard with engines revving up in the background and noise all around him.

"Listen. I don't have time for this stuff. Find somebody else." And with that he turned and walked away.

Lou was hoping to get the guy's name and address, but he lost him. Lou watched as he went over to some people and seemed to be upset over the interview. When he left, Lou approached one of the women, Lore Beyer.

"Can you tell me who that guy with the bandanna was?"

"Who wants to know?" Lore asked, a bit defensive and flexing her biceps that had tattoos of dragons on them.

"I do. He's won some money and I didn't get his name and address."

"Oh, he'll want money. His name is Jack Cady and he lives in Schaffer. Jack's our best fund raiser."

"Really?"

"Yeah, he sold the most raffle tickets for the Bay Cliff Health Camp, a camp for children with disabilities. One of his ticket buyers, a woman in Harris by the name of Rose Smith won the prize, a new Harley-Davidson."

"Good for him. Say, I didn't catch his name. Can't hear very well with all the noise around here. Would you write his name on my paper here. Put his town down there, too, will ya?" She did. Lou thanked her and headed for the fourth suspect. He couldn't find him and the other one probably had left by the time he had gotten around to the specific area where he was spotted.

Well, this was a waste of time, Lou thought. Other than being around a lot of fascinating people and beautiful bikes, he didn't feel like he got any new information, except this Jack guy might prove to be a suspect. He went back to the Capital Area SHHH Chapter to thank them for their help. As he approached, Roy Del Valle handed him a roll of film and said, "This might come in handy. Here's my card. Send me the photos you don't need. Some were pictures taken at my nephew's wedding."

"What did you take?" Lou asked.

"I took some distance shots of you talking to the two bikers," Roy said.

"Great. Thanks for your help. I appreciate it."

The next morning Lou was in a short line at the one-hour film processing counter at a local drug store. He waited till the processing was complete. He paid for the photos and then went right over to the bank when it opened on Monday morning. He talked with Lenore and showed her the photos.

"I can't tell anything from these pictures," Lenore said. "This guy could be anybody. Yeah, he has hair and seems about six feet tall, but I can't be certain he robbed our bank."

"I'll share the photos with the police. They can compare it with the bank videos and see if there's any resemblance."

"Good idea, Lou."

Lou took the photos to Sergeant Liming and suggested a trade. "I'll give you the photos for a copy of the audio tape from the bank hold up."

"You can't withhold any possible evidence in this crime, Lou."

"Oh, I know, this is simply my way of asking for a copy of the tape."

"I'll have a copy made and you can pick it up later this afternoon."

"Many thanks, Detective Liming."

Lou decided to go to Schaffer, a few miles due north of Bark River, to see if Jack Cady had a record or even a reputation with the police. The police were very cooperative but Lou didn't learn anything. Jack had no record and wasn't even recognized by the cops. Lou was about to erase Jack off his suspect list. After all, Lenore hadn't recognized him and he seemed clean in his town.

As fate would have it, a statewide conference of speech pathologists, speech scientists, and audiologists was going on in the Bottom Center at Northern Michigan Univesity. Lou arrived and asked to speak to Dr. Peter LaPine, a speech scientist from Michigan State University and a friend of his. He knew that Dr. LaPine was often called upon to testify in major trials and to participate in national and international cases of huge importance.

Professor LaPine was paged and quickly appeared with an outstretched hand.

"How can I help the famous detective?" Peter asked.

"I need your help and thankfully you're up here fairly close to where I'm tryin' to solve a crime."

"Tell me what you need, and I'll help if I can."

"I'd like you to analyze two tapes and tell me if you think the same guy is talking. You will hear a common phrase in each tape. The phrase is 'You deaf or somethin'?'"

"I can do that. You've got both tapes with you?"

"No, I'm to pick up one of the tapes from the police this afternoon."

"I'm flying back to East Lansing this evening," Professor LaPine explained. "You get me the tapes and I'll work on them in my lab tonight and call you in the morning."

"That's great. I need to know if the same guy is talking on both tapes. Oh, there is quite a bit of background noise on one tape, Professor."

"I'll see what I can do, Lou."

When Lou stopped to pick up the tape at police headquarters, he asked Sergeant Liming if it was possible to have a voice line-up.

"A voice line-up?" Ann asked.

"Yeah, you know, have six guys line up and have each of them say the same thing and see if Lenore can identify a voice."

"Sure, we can do that. Have you got a suspect?" Detective Liming asked.

"Not yet, but when I find the guy, Lenore can help by listening to what the thief said during the robbery. A visual identification won't help her. She needs to hear him talk."

"We may be able to combine the two."

"Combine the two?" Lou asked.

"Yeah, have a traditional line-up but also ask each guy to say something."

"I don't mean just saying anything. He's got to be asked to say something you have on the tape."

"We can do that, sure. I've got to have a warrant to bring in a suspect, we can't just ask him to stop in."

"I'm aware of that. If my hunch works, I'll have a suspect in twenty-four hours."

The next morning Professor LaPine called Lou. "Got a match, Lou."

"Batch of what?"

"Match, got a MATCH for you. The voice on the two tapes appears to be the same."

"Great news, Professor! You don't seem to have an ounce of doubt either."

"Well, in my business, you can't state anything with one hundred percent accuracy, but the frequencies seem to match in both voices. I'd say the voices probably belong to the same person."

"Great! Good work. You may have hit upon the piece of evidence that will solve this case!"

Lou contacted the police and reported the professor's findings and suggested a warrant be placed for the arrest of Jack Cady. The voice match, the Harley-Davidson bandanna, and his matching the description of the robber should be enough to convince a judge to issue a warrant for his arrest.

A warrant was issued, Jack was arrested and the stage was set for the voice line-up. Lenore was asked to go to the police station. She looked through a one-way mirror with a set of earphones on her head. Six men walked into the room. Jack was in the number four position. All six were about the same height with full heads of hair. Nobody seemed to catch her attention.

"I can't tell by looking at them, Lou."

"That's OK. The police will tell each of them to put the bandanna over their nose and mouth and to say the phrase, 'You deaf or somethin'.' You listen and see if you can pick out who was at your window when the bank was robbed."

"Will do my best, Lou."

Each man in the line-up was told to take the bandanna from around his neck, cover his nose and mouth with the handkerchief and then say one at a time, 'You deaf or somethin'?"

Lenore was instructed to listen carefully. After all six had said the four-word sentence, she asked Sergeant Liming if they could all repeat the short sentence. She so directed and Lenore listened. When they all had finished Lenore said to Lou, "I can't be sure. I think it was number two or maybe number six."

"OK, Lenore. Thanks for listening. Nobody seemed to jump out at you, either visually or auditorily. Is that what you're saying?"

"I can't be sure."

While Lenore was on her way back to work, Detective Liming interrogated Jack. His story seemed to hold up, so he was released, but not until he was directed to stay close to home in case more questions needed to be answered.

Jack had willingly agreed to a lie detector test and passed it with flying colors. Lou, Ann, and Dick were present. Jack was asked, "Were you at the Bark River Bank at ten a.m.?" Jack said, "No, sir, I was selling raffle tickets in Harris at ten a.m." The stylus didn't go crazy on the paper roll, which meant that Jack was probably telling the truth.

He was selling tickets in <u>Paris</u>?" Lou asked Ann in disbelief.

"No, Harris, Lou. He was selling raffle tickets in Harris, Michigan," Ann replied.

"Where's Harris?"

"A few miles west of here as the crow flies, but an hour away on your watch."

The examiner next asked, "Did you rob a bank at ten o'clock?" Once again the answer was "No, I told ya, I was selling raffle tickets for our motorcycle club. You deaf or somethin'?" and once again, the stylus remained steady.

The examiner turned to Dick and said, "I don't think this guy was in your bank, let alone the one who robbed it. These tests aren't perfect, but I think you've picked up the wrong guy."

Lou was disappointed. He felt certain he had the right man, but without Lenore's clear recognition, visual or auditory, Jack's passing a lie detector test, and without the professor being able to say without an ounce of doubt that Jack was the man behind the voice in the bank's tape, he was at a loss for where to turn.

He decided to call his audiologist friend, Dr. Hal Bate, at Western Michigan University.

"What help could I possibly give you, Lou? "Professor Bate asked.

"Actually I'm facing a brick wall. I thought I had my man but I guess I don't."

"What's the problem?"

Lou told Dr. Bate all that he knew about the case, "Professor LaPine gave me a heads-up on a match between my tape of this guy's voice and the voice on the bank tape. I was able to convince the police to seek a warrant to arrest the guy on suspicion of bank robbery. We asked Lenore, I think you know Lenore Coscarelli...."

"Yes, I know Lenore," Hal replied. "She's a marvelous advocate."

"Yes, she is. Anyway, we asked her to try and pick the guy out of a line-up. She couldn't pick out the suspect visually. Then we asked her to listen to a line the bank robber said and once again she couldn't pick out the guy. The air went out of my balloon. I thought for sure she'd say, 'That's him' and point a finger in his direction."

"I think I know the answer, but what did Lenore say was the reason she couldn't identify the man by his voice?" Hal asked.

"She said she could understand every word he said in the line-up, but in the bank she had a lot of trouble understanding what he said. She said this was not only because of her loss but also because she was denied speechreading clues."

"Yup, that's what I thought she'd say."

"Why would you say that?"

"Because when you know what's going to be said, you anticipate it, and sure enough you hear it."

"Makes sense, but explain."

"Well, if I say to you without looking at you 'Fish bite in the morning on a cloudy day,' you, with your hearing loss and hearing this sentence out of context, might hear some of it and misunderstand the rest of it."

"Yeah, I sure would."

"But, if I said, I'm going to say, 'Fish bite in the morning on a cloudy day' and then say it, you'll hear it perfectly or at least your brain will interpret what you hear as the exact sentence I said I would say."

"So, you think Lenore, in knowing what the guys were going to say, heard it all?"

"Exactly. You can't replicate the exact situation for Lenore either. So with the stress of the situation, a different setting, and the guy restating a phrase that Lenore is expecting, you can't recreate the listening and speaking situation. And, you can't be certain the suspect will use his same voice. He would probably use a slightly different voice."

"Hmmm, I understand. I thought she could simply pick his voice out of a line-up."

"Not after hearing it only once, Lou."

"Well, do you have any advice for solving this thing?"

"From all that you've told me, I'd say the answer can be found on the map."

"The answer to a guy robbing a bank can be found while I nap?" Lou asked.

"No, Lou, found on a map, MAP, the visual representation of a state's layout."

"Oh, a MAP. Why didn't you tell me you were going to say a MAP," Lou said with a smile. "You think the answer is in the map?"

"I think it is. You said he was selling raffle tickets in Harris, Michigan, and even identified who he was selling to. You also told me that you asked these people if Jack was selling raffle tickets about ten o'clock on the day of the robbery. Later, each person verified that they were buying tickets about that time."

"Must have a lot of folks who can lie, huh, Hal?" Lou said.

"Nope, they were telling the truth. You see, once Jack passed into Bark River, he went into a different time zone. The Bark River Bank was robbed at 10 a.m. when it opened. When it was ten o'clock in Bark River, it was nine in Harris." .

Lou thought and repeated what Hal had said. "So, when Jack told us he was selling tickets in Harris at ten, it was eleven in Bark River. Have I got it?" Lou asked.

"That's right," confirmed Hal. "He probably robbed the Bark River Bank and then went to Harris, which is in another time zone and at about 10 their time, eleven o'clock in Bark River, he was selling raffle tickets instead of sitting in a Bark River police squad car under arrest for robbing their bank."

"Right, Hal. No wonder you are a legend! Very good, and Jack most certainly would be telling the truth which is why he so boldly suggested a lie detector test."

Lou took Hal's theory to Sergeant Liming and it all made a lot of sense to her. Jack was arrested, given a new lie detector test and failed miserably. It is all in the questions you ask, I guess," Lou said, ready to seal another case.

"Yeah, pat on the back for you, Lou," Ann said, slapping Lou on the shoulder. "You cracked it by finding the guy at the 'Bless the Bikes' rally in Escanaba."

"I simply put two and two together," Lou replied humbly. "Lenore gets all the credit for stalling him, getting him to talk and giving the police time to get there."

"Well, you two take the credit then," Detective Liming said with her classic smile. "Guess we have that speech science professor and that audiology professor to thank for some great help."

"Yeah, it was a team effort. Hal really tipped me off when he said the solution was all in the map. Oh, let me ask, did you ever get his reason for robbing the bank?"

"Yeah, he said he wanted to pay for hearing aids for his mother. She doesn't have any insurance and really needs the aids," Ann replied.

"All he had to do was ask and we'd get him all the help he needed."

"I guess you can still do that," Sergeant Liming said. "Thanks to Lenore he didn't get much money. He'll turn most if not all of it in and he'll probably plea bargain and get some community service time and be put on probation. He might get some jail time, but if he does, it won't be a lot. He's got no record. I think he simply lost good judgment for a minute. He's no professional thief. He simply wanted to help his mother and didn't know how best to do it."

Epilogue

Part of Jack's community service was to lead a fundraising project for the Capital Area SHHH Chapter. A raffle was held and enough money was raised to get hearing aids for Jack's mother. Oh, and by the way, Jack's mother joined a SHHH Chapter and received much help from the many folks who shared her hearing problem.

The End

THE SEARING MYSTERIES

Your Hearing Aids or Your Life!

THE SEARING MYSTERIES

The dead body was discovered early Sunday morning because of the incessant barking of a dog. Guests of the Radisson Hotel in St. Paul, Minnesota, didn't expect to have their privacy interrupted by the non-stop barking of an undisciplined dog in Room 545. Several guests called the front desk to complain.

The front desk clerk asked the supervisor to see if the dog was alone or with an owner. The housekeeping supervisor knocked several times but received no answer. She opened the door and there on the floor at the base of the bed, lay a fully-clothed woman by the name of Judy Watkins. A knife was stuck in her back. The dog stopped barking but stayed close to his owner and appeared quite disturbed.

The room was not ransacked. Everything appeared to be in its place. Judy's purse was on the small desk. All credit cards and cash were in the purse. The jewelry was still on the body or in an unlocked jewelry bag in her luggage. The initial belief of the St. Paul Police Detective, Rocky Stone was that the death was the result of some type of personal conflict. Since nothing was stolen, the murder could not be attributed to Judy's surprising a thief.

The police quickly learned from the hotel staff that the room was occupied by Judy Watkins of Albuquerque, New Mexico, and Lyndz Fortune of North Carolina. The two women apparently didn't know one another before agreeing to share a room at the Self Help for Hard of Hearing People's annual convention.

Hotel records indicated that Lyndz had checked out late Saturday afternoon. When a call was placed to her home to verify her whereabouts, Lyndz answered the phone. She was no help in explaining who killed Judy or why the murder occurred. She reported she said "Good-bye" to Judy late Saturday before checking out and taking a cab to the airport.

Most of the participants of the SHHH Convention in St. Paul, Minnesota, had already left the Radisson Hotel. Several members had chosen to take a one day post-convention trip to Duluth. A handful of staff whose job it was to take care of convention wrap-up details were also in the hotel.

Needless to say, word spread quickly that a woman had been murdered on the fifth floor. The worst thing that can happen to a hotel is a murder. The manager could do nothing to stop the rumors of the crisis and like a wildfire fueled by strong breezes, the news went through the Radisson Hotel located on Kellogg Boulevard.

The paramedics and emergency personnel as well as police, detectives, and photographers entered the hotel through the delivery entrance on the east side. The fifth floor was immediately declared off limits to anyone not having any responsibility at the crime scene. All guests were moved to rooms on other floors and allowed to gather their belongings under the watchful eyes of hotel personnel and the police.

Judy's body was removed from the room once the medical examiner had done his work, the police photographer had taken sufficient pictures of the crime scene, and Sergeant Stone was assured that all evidence had been collected. The body was taken to the ambulance via an 'Employees Only' elevator and then taken to the morgue where an autopsy would be performed.

Michigan private investigator and mystery writer Lou Searing had been attending the convention. He had also been scheduled to return to Michigan, but when he learned that bad weather was causing flight cancellations, he decided to stay one more night and leave in the morning. When Lou learned about Judy's death, he immediately made his services available to the St. Paul Police.

Detective Stone was not interested in having a private investigator get involved. Lou understood this and really couldn't blame him for his attitude. The problem was that Lou felt compelled to get involved; after all, a fellow member of the SHHH was dead and he wanted to find out who had killed her. There wasn't a force strong enough to keep Lou away from trying to bring justice to this tragedy.

Judy Watkins was an advocate for hard of hearing people in New Mexico. She coordinated SHHH activities in the Southwest. Her hearing loss was a result of meningitis a few years ago. She had recently been evaluated for a cochlear implant, a procedure that was expected to significantly improve her reception of sound. In the meantime she had worn two behind-the-ear hearing aids. Judy was a good example of a person with hearing loss who took advantage of current technology to communicate effectively with others.

Judy and her border collie hearing dog, Clever, were constant companions, and were usually in the front row of sessions that caught Judy's interest. Whenever Judy would tell someone about her hearing dog and all the unique skills he possessed, the listener would say, "Well, isn't that clever!" So, Judy decided to name her dog Clever, and for the past six years, the two had been inseparable.

Judy was seen in the research symposium on Saturday morning. A videotape of the session showed Judy in a colorful dress asking a question and contemplating a response. She was also seen having lunch at the Subway sandwich shop down the street from the hotel. And, she had attended the SHHH banquet on Saturday evening. She sat with friends she had gotten to know during the convention. Nothing had seemed to be bothering her.

What to do with Clever was a problem. Lou decided the only humane thing to do was to take the dog and care for him until another owner could be found. Lou and his wife, Carol, had two cats, Luba and Millie, and a golden retriever named Samm. Lou liked dogs so he decided to care for Clever, it was the least he could do. Clever seemed to take to Lou, licking his face and constantly sticking close to him.

It was hard to know where to begin. Lou decided to start by contacting members of Judy's family to see what conflicts she may have been having in her life. That turned into a dead end when he learned that Judy was a very compassionate person and everyone adored her. No family member could think of anyone who would do this. This was one of those classic stories where the victim didn't have an enemy in the world.

Early Sunday morning, Lou got permission from Sergeant Stone to inspect Judy's belongings. The clothes did not interest him, but he did want to see her personal items. The bag was clearly marked, "Personal items on the body." Inside the plastic bag were a ring, a necklace, and two earrings. A pair of glasses was also in the bag. But two obvious items that should have been in the bag were missing, Judy's hearing aids.

Lou looked at other evidence thinking the hearing aids were knocked off during the murder and perhaps were found in the area of the body. He looked at the list of items found in her purse and there were no hearing aids on the list. He also checked the list of suitcase contents and the items in her cosmetic bag, but no hearing aids. *Hmmm. That's strange,* Lou thought. *Why would her hearing aids be missing? Nobody would kill for a couple of hearing aids.* There had to be some mistake or they were overlooked by the St. Paul Police.

It was Sunday and Lou had not gone to church in the morning because of his work in investigating the murder. He decided to go to afternoon Mass at the Cathedral. Clever needed some exercise so the two of them took the twenty minute walk to church. He knew having a hearing dog was legal in a church but he didn't want any undue attention to Clever so he slipped in and sat in an aisle seat in the back of the church.

All went well until the people began to move around, getting in line for Communion. Clever seemed agitated and couldn't seem to relax as people left their pews to get into the slow moving line. Suddenly, Clever seemed to go crazy with incessant barking and yapping at the feet of a middle-aged gentleman who stepped back and gave Lou an ugly stare. Lou was thoroughly embarrassed as Clever's barks were obviously causing hundreds of heads to turn in his direction. Lou scooped Clever up and quickly exited the side door, but in doing so realized that Clever was obviously disturbed at something he had seen, smelled or sensed.

Lou quickly determined that the man was the reason for Clever's inappropriate outburst. He could see his face in a flashback to the embarrassing experience. The man was about six feet tall, thin, and completely bald. He was wearing a suit. One of Lou's techniques for remembering a person was to see if he could imagine a look alike. He bore a strong resemblance to a young Yul Brynner in "The King and I." Lou also noticed that he was wearing two behind-the-ear hearing aids.

Lou wrapped Clever's leash around a small tree and went back into the church. Back and forth his eyes went trying to locate the gentleman with the nice-looking suit. Suddenly, there he was in Lou's field of vision. He seemed alone. Lou stared long and hard trying to recall every detail in his sight. Lou took a seat in the very last pew and never let the suspect out of his sight. There was some reason for Clever to be upset and this man very well could have something to do with Judy's murder.

The Mass ended, a final hymn was sung, and the procession slowly made its way to the back of the church.

The man in the suit rose, crossed himself, genuflected in the aisle in the direction of the Tabernacle, turned and walked toward the back door of the Cathedral. Lou kept him in sight and then all of a sudden two women approached Lou and began talking about his cute dog and telling him not to be embarrassed. Lou was polite and thanked the ladies for their kind remarks, but in the few seconds he was distracted by these two elderly women, he lost the suspect who melded into the congregation exiting the church.

Lou quickly went outside to see if he could see the man, but he couldn't. The suspect had gotten away leaving Lou to wonder if he really had something to do with Judy's murder or perhaps Clever just didn't like the guy or was startled by his spit-polished shoes or the aroma of some aftershave lotion. Lou might have stumbled onto a major clue while on his knees in church, but if he had, it had eluded him.

Lou walked to the small tree restraining Clever who by now was relaxed and almost sleeping. Lou unwrapped the leash and began the short walk back to the Radisson on Kellogg Boulevard. For the duration of the trip, Clever walked along as if all was normal once again.

When Lou got back to the Radisson, the bus from the tour to Duluth was unloading passengers. Lou recognized several of the SHHH members who seemed a bit tired from the long trip. He saw Barbara Thomas, a member of the SHHH staff in Bethesda. Lou knew that Barbara was a friend of Judy's and would be devastated with the news of the murder. "Hi Lou, what are you doing with Clever?"

"I need to talk to you, Barbara. I have some bad news so you'd better sit down."

"Oh, no. I don't want to hear this," Barbara said, quickly deducting that something had happened to Judy.

"Judy has been murdered. She was found dead in her room on the fifth floor."

"Oh, my goodness. Why, Lou?"

"I don't know. I've been working on it most of the day. She was stabbed in the back, but nothing of value was taken. By the way, her family is coming to St. Paul, but doesn't know who could have done this. I inspected all of her belongings but the only thing missing was her hearing aids."

"Hearing aids? Why would anyone want her hearing aids?" Barbara asked.

"I have no idea. They're getting kind of expensive, but hardly worth killing for."

"The missing hearing aids may have had nothing to do with this, Lou. Maybe Judy was involved in something sinister."

"Not likely, but yes, she could have been harboring a dark secret that nobody knows about."

"Judy was such a wonderful person. I don't think she was involved in something sinister. I can't get over this."

"Yes, it's disturbing. But, on occasion I've heard of victims who had things going on in their lives that shocked family and friends once it was revealed."

"Do you suspect anyone at the convention, Lou?" Barbara asked.

"I don't have any suspects at this point. I just got back from church and while I was there, Clever went ballistic when a tall, bald man in a suit came down the aisle for Communion. I lost him in the crowd after church. Unless he was an out-of-town guest, he'll be back and I'll try to spot him again and then track him."

"In the meantime what are you going to do?"

"Study evidence, follow leads and ask questions, I guess."

"If you don't have dinner plans, several of us are going out after we freshen up a bit from our trip to Duluth. Would you like to join us?"

"Thanks. I'd like the company. Can I bring Clever with me?"

"Absolutely."

"Who'll be going to dinner?"

"Let's see. I think we'll be going with Michael Bower, Ken Goodmiller, Harriet Frankel, Mark Rosing, Penny Allen, Linda Lundeen Moen, Nancy Wright and Pat Vincent. We've got quite a group. We enjoyed each other's company on the Duluth trip. You'll like them. They might even be able to help you with your investigation."

That evening Lou sat down to dinner in the Sunken Gardens Chinese Restaurant in St. Paul. After ordering, Lou asked those around him about their trip to Duluth.

After a few minutes the talk turned to Judy's murder. Ken Goodmiller of Fincastle, Virginia, interrupted and said, 'I've not heard anything about this, but I'll bet she was found dead in her room." Lou was surprised that Ken would know this detail.

"One of my many psychic powers, Lou." Ken said with a wink.

Lou, still intrigued by Ken's accurate comment told them about the investigation so far. Several people seemed to have a possible scenario. Lou listened and took notes because each theory had credibility and as silly as a few seemed to be, each comment had the potential to assist in solving the case.

Michael Bower started by saying that Clever might have eaten the aids.

"Oh, no way!" Lou exclaimed, finding the suggestion ludicrous.

"No, really, it has happened on more than one occasion. The dog starts playing with the aid, nibbling at it, then chewing, and finally the hearing aid is in the dog's body."

Linda Lundeen Moen of St. Paul added, "It happens, Lou. My hearing dog, previous to the one I have now, really did eat my hearing aid!"

"Hmmm, I suppose that could account for the missing hearing aids," Lou said.

Penny Allen of Port Orchard, Washington, spoke up. "I lost my hearing aids one day and I looked all over the house and couldn't find them. I had purchased some colorful aids and they happened to be the same color as my bedspread.

Did you look carefully on the bed, Lou?"

"No, I didn't, but the police are very skilled in evidence-gathering and I would imagine they would have found them if they were on the bedspread. That's a good point. I'll look into that, Penny. Thanks."

Harriet Frankel spoke up next. "If she had a roommate, that person could have taken them by mistake. I was rooming with two others at this conference and one morning, I couldn't find my glasses and it turned out that one of the other women had taken my glasses by mistake. So, maybe that is what happened?"

"That could be it, but I talked to her roommate, Lyndz Fortune, and she didn't mention that she had her hearing aids. I'll call again and ask. Thanks."

Nancy Wright from Michigan told about the time she took her hearing aid off and put it in one of those travel bags with a zillion little compartments. "I thought I'd lost my aid but after I opened one of those many little zippered parts of the bag, I found it."

"Good suggestion," I replied. "We'll do a thorough check of her luggage and cosmetic bag. Thanks, Nancy."

"Any other thoughts?" Lou asked.

Mark Rosing of Cincinnati, Ohio spoke up. "You know, you might check Judy's pockets. Sometimes we hard of hearing people put our hearing aids in shirt pockets to give our ears a break and her aids might still be in her pocket."

"That's a thought, Mark. Thanks. Anyone else?"

"I'm Pat Vincent from Grove City, Ohio, Lou. I don't have any idea where the aids may have gone, but I will suggest that when this murder is solved, the hearing dog will have had a major part to play. Hearing dogs are very smart and while they can't talk, they do communicate. Watch that dog, Clever, because he really is, Lou." All around the dinner table nodded at Pat's statement.

The meal was enjoyed and Lou realized how thankful he was to know such wonderful people in the SHHH organization and from all over the country, too.

When Lou got back to his room he noticed the red light blinking on his phone. He listened to the message. It was from Detective Sergeant Stone who asked him to call.

"Detective, this is Lou Searing returning your call."

"Thanks for calling, Lou. I wanted you to know that we've been alerted that a smuggling operation is underway in the Twin Cities. Apparently diamonds worth millions of dollars were taken from a prestigious jewelry store in New York. Our sources say that with Northwest Airlines having a hub in Minneapolis, it could be a center for moving these diamonds. Doubt it has anything to do with the murder at the Radisson but wanted you to know."

"Thanks for letting me in on this, Sergeant. I agree. A diamond smuggling operation would not be the reason for the murder of Judy Watkins. I say this because nothing was taken from the room, not even Judy's diamond ring, and it was a rock, too."

"Where are you at the moment, Lou?"

"I'm at the Radisson in downtown St. Paul."

"Which one?"

"Which one what?"

"Which Radisson?"

"I don't know. You mean there's more than one Radisson Hotel in downtown St. Paul?"

"Yes, there are two Radisson Hotels in St. Paul about six blocks apart. There is City Center Hotel on Minneapolis Street and the other is on Kellogg Boulevard."

"I'm in the one closest to the river, I guess."

"That's the one on Kellogg."

"Right. Listen, thanks for the call."

"You're welcome."

"I owe you some sharing, Detective Stone. Judy Watkins had a hearing dog, a border collie named Clever. I took responsibility for him and yesterday afternoon, in the St. Paul Cathedral up on the hill, west of downtown, this dog went bananas when he spotted a guy coming down the aisle for Communion. Clever is usually a very mild-mannered dog so I'm sure seeing this guy was related to the murder."

"Interesting. What happened?"

"I wanted to follow the man but lost him in the crowd leaving church."

"Sounds like you were fairly close to a murderer, Lou."

"Yeah, I think I was. I got a good look at him. He was wearing two hearing aids."

"Give me a good description and I'll relay the information so our officers can be on the alert for him."

"He was about six feet tall, bald, wearing two behind-the-ear hearing aids, nicely dressed. He bares a strong resemblance to a young Yul Brynner."

"Got it, thanks. He could have been attending your convention."

"Yeah, I guess he could've. There were several hundred people milling around the hotel. I looked at a lot of people over the past few days and never saw this guy, but yeah, he could have been at the convention."

"Well, let's keep in touch."

"Yes, we will."

Lou no more than hung up the phone when it rang. "Mr. Searing?"

"Speaking."

"This is Lyndz Fortune. I told you I had no information about Judy's murder, but I remembered something that happened."

"What might that be, Lyndz?"

"Well, I went to our room and saw the blinking red message light. I didn't know if it would be for me or for Judy. I picked up the phone and listened."

"What did you hear?"

"It was strange. It went something like this, 'Room number 545, this is Minneapolis-St. Paul. Transfer tomorrow morning.'"

"You're sure that was the message?"

"Yes, it was so strange that I listened to a replay."

"Did you tell Judy about the message?" Lou asked.

"Yes, and it didn't make sense to her either."

"Thanks for sharing this information and if you think

of anything else that you heard or saw, don't hesitate to call me."

"OK, Lou. I hope you solve this soon."

Lou analyzed the message and two things caught his attention. The first was "Room 545" and the second was "Transfer tomorrow morning." Since Judy's hearing aids were not listed among the items found on her body, Lou deducted that the murder had to have involved her hearing aids. Other than her missing hearing aids, he couldn't figure out what else would be transferred.

Lou realized a critical part of the message was room number 545. Since he had learned that there were two Radisson Hotels in downtown St. Paul and less than six blocks apart, he thought the two hotels could have been confused and the transfer of hearing aids was really meant to occur at the other Radisson. If he were right, Judy would find herself involved in a smuggling operation that might have had nothing to do with her. Otherwise, Judy <u>was</u> involved in a crime ring and something had gone wrong.

The next day, Lou decided to take Clever and go to the Mall of America. Every first-time visitor to Minneapolis needs to see the largest mall in the world, if not to shop, then to see the acres and acres of retail shops, food courts, and the myriad of activities for children. Lou had no lead to pursue and he had a little time on his hands, so he and Clever headed for a city bus that would take them for a 20-minute ride to the Mall of America, located south of Minneapolis.

The bus ride was uneventful and before Lou and Clever knew it, they were pulling into a bus terminal on the east side of the mall. Lou inquired about return times, got off the bus, and followed the signs into the Mall. What he found was a shopping mall gone crazy. People were going into and out of hundreds of retail shops. With Clever on a leash, he made his way along aisles in front of every kind of store one could imagine on many levels of the mall. He really had no goal in mind, except to purchase a Harley-Davidson T-shirt if he happened upon one. Lou wanted to say that he had been to the Mall of America, the largest symbol of capitalism found in the Midwest, if not in the US of A.

After an hour plus of walking, window shopping, and having children admire Clever, Lou stopped at a food court for a bite to eat. He purchased his order and sat down at a table. Lou got a cup of water for Clever and put down a few Milk Bones. The two were enjoying the break when once again Clever went crazy with incessant barking.

Lou realized immediately that Clever had undoubtedly seen something that bothered him. He had a flashback to the Mass yesterday when Clever got so upset when the man with the hearing aids walked past them on his way to Communion.

Lou looked in the direction where Clever was fixed on something or someone. He couldn't see anything out of the ordinary but kept watching. An inside-the-Mall roller coaster ride was coming to an end and people were about to get off when Clever intensified his barking to the point that many people were looking at him and wondering why Lou couldn't control his dog.

Then Lou saw him, the same man from church, walking out of the roller coaster ride's ticket and boarding center. He glanced up toward Lou and Clever and realized that he had been spotted again. He moved quickly out of the area. Lou left the food court and tried to follow the man. There were so many people in the Mall, there was no way he could track him.

Lou decided to take the chance of a reprimand by unhooking the leash and letting Clever go. He figured Clever would seek out the man and once again go crazy with barking, and all Lou had to do was to go to the barking sound. So, he unhooked the leash and off scampered Clever.

Lou followed and remained on the lookout for a security guard or better yet, a police officer. If Clever was able to find the man and if the police could get to him in time, he might have a suspect in the murder. Because by now, Lou was convinced that the man had been in Judy's room and had in fact killed her.

Since Clever was not a bloodhound and couldn't see higher than a foot or two off the ground, the man got away. Lou did find a police officer and explained the situation. The officer radioed a call for security in the Mall to be looking for a stylishly dressed bald man last seen on the second level near the food court and roller coaster ride, heading east. Eventually Lou found Clever, a bit tired for all of his barking and a failed chase.

Lou decided to head back to the Radisson. Lou and Clever boarded the bus and had an uneventful stop and go ride through the streets of St. Paul. Back at the hotel Lou decided to rest for a bit and ponder what he knew so far. He couldn't seem to get the potential confusion between the two Radissons off his mind. He needed to try to discover if there was a connection between the two.

The phone rang and it was Detective Stone. "One of our officers spotted the bald gentleman who resembles a young Yul Brynner."

"That's good news. Where?"

"He was exiting a cab and went into the Embassy Suites Hotel on 10th Street."

"Hmmm, I think I'll take Clever there and see what happens. Can you join me?"

"Yeah, I can meet you there. I'll not be in uniform, however."

"Fine. I just want to see if Clever goes out of control should the guy walk through the lobby."

Sergeant Stone thought he'd have a weak case for obtaining a search warrant in the event the man was sighted. He really did not have enough evidence to arrest the man for murder or to get permission from the prosecutor to search the man's room. After all, the only evidence they had was a barking dog. Perhaps if he could present the theory in a convincing manner, the prosecuting attorney would agree with him that the police couldn't risk losing this man.

About 7 o'clock that evening, Lou and Clever walked into the Embassy Suites Hotel on 10th Street. Detective Stone was in plainclothes and seated in a lounge chair in the hotel lobby. Lou and Clever sat nearby, opposite the elevator doors. A good hour went by with no sighting. Lou realized this could go on for hours. After all, the man may not even be in this hotel.

Lou walked over to the registration desk and asked to speak to the manager. The manager came out from the back and said, "Can I help you?"

"Yes, do you have a guest in this hotel who is a Yul Brynner look-alike?"

"Yes, we sure do. Most people who see him think he has come back to life. Why, may I ask?"

"I talked to this man earlier today about hearing aids. I wear them and so does he. I told him about my hearing dog. He said he'd like to see him. But after we parted I realized I hadn't gotten his name—just where he was staying. I was hoping to talk to him about my dog."

"I see."

"Can you give me his room number?" Lou asked.

"No, we don't give our guests' room numbers out."

"Sure, I understand. Thanks."

"But I can tell you that he spends time in the bar every night."

"Really?"

"Yeah, you can find him in there from around 11 p.m. till closing and that's about 2 a.m."

"Thanks. I'll stop back and perhaps I can convince him to get a hearing dog. Thanks for your help."

Lou walked over to Detective Stone and told him what he had learned. He suggested he take Clever back to the Kellogg Street Radisson and that the two of them come back around midnight.

It was about ten to midnight when Lou and Rocky Stone walked into the lounge. They had gone over their plan to lure the man into their trap. Lou believed the suspect didn't have a hearing loss. He would try to get both aids off of him. If he could get hold of the hearing aids, he might be able to tell if they were real or just for show. He would also ask him questions only a hearing aid wearer could answer and questions he wouldn't be able to hear without his aids on. He and Detective Stone would soon be able to ascertain if they had reason to suspect him of Judy's murder.

Lou and Sergeant Stone sat down at a table and ordered a drink. They seemed to be in deep conversation when in reality they were looking at every patron and discussing whether any of them could be Judy's killer.

Lou was the first to recognize the suspect. He was at the bar with a couple of women, talking and sipping a drink. Lou called the waiter over and said, "We'd like to buy a drink for that guy at the bar talking to the two women. Let him know that a fellow hearing aid wearer is buying him a drink."

"Sure. Will do."

A few minutes later, the gentleman looked over at them. He excused himself from the women, got off the bar stool, and headed toward Lou. "I understand I have you two to thank for a drink. Something about bonding over hearing loss?"

"Yeah, I wear hearing aids and we noticed that you wear a couple of aids so we thought we'd do our good deed for the day and offer you a drink."

"Thanks. Do I know you folks?"

"I doubt it. My name's Lou and this is Rocky."

"Nice to meet you. I'm Taylor."

"What kind of hearing aid do you wear, Taylor?" Lou asked.

"I don't know. Never paid any attention."

"Can I see one?"

"I guess so." Taylor said, taking his aid off and placing it on the table."

Lou picked it up and noticed it was heavier than it should be. "This is a powerful baby. Do you like your aids?" Lou asked.

"Yeah, they work okay for me."

"Let me see the other one, do you mind?"

"Guess not." The second aid was placed on the table.

Lou purposefully knocked his glasses case on the floor and while he was leaning over to pick it up he said quietly, "Where you from, Taylor?"

"Chicago. Here for a few days on business."

Still fiddling around for his glasses case, Lou asked his next question at a sound level where only a normal-hearing person could hear. "What kind of batteries do you use, Taylor?"

"Can't tell you. My wife handles all of that. I just put one in whenever I need one."

"How often do you have to change them?" Lou asked, sitting upright once again and convinced that Taylor had no hearing loss whatsoever.

"Never paid much attention. Every couple of days, I suppose."

As Lou tapped Sergeant Stone's leg with the tip of his shoe, he said, "You don't get much life from these powerful little batteries."

Detective Stone, who had been quiet up to now, flashed his badge and said. "You're under arrest for murder." He began to read the Miranda rights when Taylor interrupted.

"Are you nuts? That's ridiculous."

"I don't think so. I believe that on Sunday morning you went to Room 545 in the Radisson Hotel on Kellogg Street to obtain stolen diamonds being transported in hearing aid casings. When you got there the woman in the room tried to convince you that she knew nothing about the diamonds but you didn't believe her. You killed her, took her hearing aids and left. Later when you opened the

. . . .

casings, you discovered she had been telling the truth. You then met your contact in Room 545 of the Radisson on <u>Minneapolis</u> Street and got the diamonds.

"You thought you were Scot free, but you didn't count on Judy's hearing dog. He recognized you twice—once in the Cathedral and again in the Mall of America. Thanks to him and some deductive reasoning we were able to find you."

At that point, Detective Stone continued reading him the Miranda Rights. Rocky then called for back up to take him to the station for booking.

"I want a lawyer, that's what I want."

"You'll get one soon enough," Detective Stone replied.

Taylor was taken to the police station, booked, and brought before a judge. A warrant led to a search of Taylor's hotel room where millions of dollars of diamonds were found. They also found a few empty hearing aid casings and directions for obtaining the smuggled gems.

The earmolds were found in Taylor's room and the ear wax from the earmolds was analyzed for DNA. Judy's earmold was one of the ones in Taylor's possession. The smuggling ring had been broken, Judy's murderer identified and Clever was a hero.

Epilogue

The jury eventually returned guilty verdicts against Taylor and others in the ring. They were sentenced to years in prison and most of the recovered diamonds were returned to New York.

The End

THE SEARING MYSTERIES

SHHH,
I Hear A Murder!

David and Jeanette Switzer were seated in The Wharton Center on the campus of Michigan State University waiting for the opening act of the Broadway musical, *Dr. Jekyll and Mr. Hyde*. David had a moderate to severe hearing loss which was the result of measles when he was little more than an infant, sixty-odd years ago. To assist him in hearing the performance, he had checked out a Phonic Ear Easy Listening device from the theater manager's office. David was required to leave his driver's license in the office as an incentive to return the device.

As people were coming into the theater, finding their seats and looking over the playbill, David was placing the headphones over his ears and turning on the device. He heard nothing as the system's activating switch had not been turned on.

The Switzers stood to let people pass into their row. David looked around trying to see if he recognized anyone in the audience. He didn't. A stranger who seemed a bit curious about David's amplifier was seated next to him. He introduced himself as Patrick Vaughan.

The auditorium was almost full and was buzzing with conversation when David heard the audio system go on. He heard some voices but they were not clear enough to understand what was being said. He also heard some backstage noise which he interpreted to be posturing of sets and a final check of props.

Jeanette pointed to an ad in the playbill, trying to get David's attention when he said, "Shhh, please. I think I hear someone being murdered."

"A murder? What on earth are you talking about?" Jeanette asked.

"A murder. I heard someone gasping for air, choking, and a voice, a threatening voice."

"Well, if you did, I'm sure they're just practicing a scene. After all this is *Dr. Jekyll and Mr. Hyde*."

"Didn't sound like a rehearsal, Jeanette. Sounded like murder."

"With your imagination being so vivid, I'm sure you thought you heard it, but with your hearing loss and a play that involves death, my guess is your imagination is on overdrive."

The lights began to dim and everyone heard the traditional welcome from the theater manager. He announced the sponsor for the performance and a change in the actors. "Ladies and gentlemen. The part of Lance, usually played by Donald Trap, will be played this evening by Hector Higgins. Thank you."

"I'll bet he was the guy who was murdered," David whispered.

Jeanette smiled and nodded thinking that this was not the place or time to confront David and his imagination. *If that's what he wants to believe, let him have his obstinate opinion*, Jeanette thought.

David knew the show business motto, "The Show Must Go On!" and doubted he would hear the siren of an approaching police vehicle or an ambulance. Because of his hearing loss and wearing the headphones, David didn't hear what others in the auditorium heard, the faint but obvious sirens from emergency vehicles.

The first scene was performed to perfection by the actors and actresses in the touring company. In fact, even David's mind settled into the story as he momentarily forgot about the choking sound and the gasp for air he had heard fifteen or twenty minutes ago. But, then the thought started to nag him. He removed his headphones and whispered to Jeanette, "I should leave and report what I heard."

"No, you don't. You'd disturb everyone in our row and those behind us, too."

"But, I heard a murder!" David replied, with his whisper almost becoming audible.

"You didn't hear a murder! Now, don't embarrass yourself and me by getting up and leaving."

David was basically a shy man and one sensitive to people's opinions and so he stayed seated and even began to believe that maybe he hadn't heard the sounds of a murder.

The producer found Donald Trap on the floor of the dressing room a few minutes before showtime. When he couldn't rouse him, he called 911 on his cell phone asking emergency personnel to come to the stage door behind the theater. He was fairly certain Donald was dead. He told the director that Donald was ill, had fainted, and for the stand-in to prepare for the performance. He didn't want to alarm the cast and crew and certainly didn't want to announce that a cast member was dead.

The police and paramedics entered the back door of the theater and went to a dressing room where they found the strangled body of the actor, Donald Trap. The paramedics found no sign of life. Red strangulation marks around Donald's neck indicated that he had met with foul play. The police photographer was taking pictures, technicians were dusting for prints and Detective Sergeant Todd Hobbs was talking to the producer, trying to get a handle on a motive and a suspect or two.

"Have any idea who could have done this?" the detective asked the producer.

"Well, he wasn't a popular guy, that's for sure. But no one jumps to my mind."

"The guy's wallet is still in his pocket. He's wearing a Rolex watch and a diamond studded ring so I doubt robbery was the motive," Detective Hobbs observed. "Strange, these look like personal items. I didn't think actors would have their personal items on while performing."

"They are personal items and normally that's the case, but actors have superstitions and idiosyncracies like anyone else. Donald didn't trust anyone and always wanted whatever was valuable to be in his possession. Since they weren't obvious things and didn't conflict with his portrayal of Lance, I didn't care if he wore them."

"Hmmm," said the detective, as he made an entry in his notebook about a lack of trust of fellow cast members.

"Donald wasn't liked, as I said. It's going to be hard to point to someone in particular because everyone despised the guy."

"Why didn't people like him?" Detective Hobbs asked.

"You know I really don't know. He was just the kind of guy that people didn't like. I think he may have crossed a couple of folks."

"Any strangers backstage in the past half hour?" asked the detective.

"Absolutely not. We've got a tight security system here. Even if someone were inside, he'd never have gotten out. Every door is guarded and there are no windows backstage."

"You said, 'HE'D never'—do you suspect a man?"

"Oh, no, I was just saying that to refer to a person. No, I don't have a suspect for you," said the producer.

David was between a rock and a hard place. He felt he needed to report to someone, if only an usher, that he'd heard what he thought to be a murder. But Jeanette was right, he probably shouldn't rise and excuse himself past twenty some people without a sound reason for doing so. His ears were not good ones and perhaps he didn't hear what he thought he heard so he remained seated.

During the first act, Raoul Garcia, the murderer, realized that his head microphone may have been turned on when he killed Donald. A wave of panic spread through his body. Raoul had planned the murder so well, but he momentarily forgot that sounds may have been sent out into the audience and into the ears of anyone wearing an assistive listening device.

As soon as Raoul was off stage he asked a stagehand to go to the manager's office and get the name and address of anyone who checked out an amplification system. The stagehand learned that only one device was checked out. It was loaned to David Switzer who lived at 1635 Sunnydale Lane in Okemos, Michigan. Raoul was not sure if his deadly deed was committed while on live mike, but if it were, and if this person heard it, he'd be the only witness to the murder.

The first act ended and for the first time the full cast learned that the dressing room had been sealed off to everyone but the police. A rumor started that Donald was more than ill. In fact, he may have been murdered, but there was no way the rumor could be verified. The medical examiner had arrived and was at work. The body would not be removed from the theater until he had finished and that could be well into the second act.

During the intermission, David rose with most theater patrons and walked toward the side aisle to move about and get some refreshments. So he wouldn't need to carry his listening device out into the lobby, Jeanette offered to put it in her purse.

Once the two of them reached the aisle and began walking to the lobby, David turned to Jeanette and said, "I'll be back. I've simply got to say something to some-body." Jeanette nodded and shrugged her shoulders. Obviously, David couldn't rest until he had gotten this off his chest.

David walked past the drinking fountain and went to a public phone located in the lower lobby of the theater. He dialed the police station, pushed the loudness button on the phone and waited for someone to answer.

"I'd like to talk to someone about a possible murder in the Wharton Center."

"This is Detective Nan Asher. How can I help you?"

"My name is David Switzer and I'm at the Wharton Center. I have a hearing loss and checked out a personal amplification system. Just before the performance, when the actors' mikes were turned on, I heard sounds that led me to believe I was listening to a murder being committed."

"Tell me more, Mr. Switzer," Sergeant Asher said. "What did you hear?"

"I heard a threatening voice. I couldn't hear the exact words because of my hearing loss, but the tone of the voice was threatening."

"Was the voice male or female?"

"It was a male voice."

"What else did you hear?"

"I heard a choking sound and some gasping is the best way to describe it."

"Ok, anything else?"

"Yes, I heard a thump, perhaps a body falling to the floor."

"Okay. Let me get some information from ...."

David saw a hand appear before him and a finger pushed down on the phone cradle. As soon as the phone went dead David felt a sharp pain in his lower back and he heard a voice behind him, "You are wanted backstage." The voice belonged to Renee Hart, an actress in the production and the murderer's accomplice. "You're to tell anyone who asks that you are a doctor summoned by the director. Do you understand?"

"I can't understand what you're saying. I've got a hearing loss."

Renee, a short woman with makeup and an obvious member of the cast was standing close behind him with a coat over her arm shielding a short, but deadly-looking knife that was touching David's back . Renee spoke up, "You're wanted backstage. Tell anyone who asks that you are a doctor summoned by the director. You're to stay with me at all times. Do you understand?"

"My wife will wonder where I am."

"She's in our custody and I assure you, if you don't cooperate, she won't see another play. Do you understand?"

"Yes."

"There is to be no commotion. Just walk with me. Believe me, any attempts to get away will bring death to your wife."

David walked alongside Renee and did as he was directed. The two walked through the crowd to the stage door. The security man recognized Renee, questioned David's entrance, but accepted that David was a doctor and let him in. The two walked to the laundry room where Renee knocked three times. On the door was a handwritten sign, "No entrance allowed until after the performance—The Management." The door opened and David was shoved in. The door was locked behind him and he was immediately tied in a chair and a sash from a robe was tightly tied around his mouth.

In the meantime, the police detective who had taken David's call was en route to the Wharton Center. Using her cell phone, she called the Wharton Center and asked to speak to the manager.

"This is Sergeant Asher with the MSU police. I was on the phone a minute ago with a Mr. Switzer who is attending the performance at your theater. I need to find him."

"This is strange. I received a request for information about this person a few minutes ago. One moment please." The manager, Kent Landsberg, sat before his computer and pulled up the patrons information page. He saw "Mr. and Mrs. Switzer" and noted the location of their seats. "I have them in the computer and their season tickets are for row 'R' in seats 26 and 27. Would you like us to send someone for him?"

"Yes, please. If he isn't in his seat, I must know immediately."

"I'll get back to you."

"Actually I'm about to arrive at the Center. I'll come to your office."

Mr. Landsberg went into the theater and found empty seats in row 'R,' seats 26 and 27. But because it was still intermission he didn't know if the Switzers were out in the hall, in restrooms, or outside the theater. The manager waited for the lights to dim and then checked again. Seat 27 was empty, but he did notice a woman in seat 26 who was constantly looking back toward the theater entrance as if she were expecting someone to appear.

Patrick Vaughan, the man in the seat next to where David was sitting, leaned over and said to Jeanette, "Excuse me. I noticed your husband's using an amplification device. I've got a hearing loss. Could I try it out until he gets back?"

"Sure," Jeanette said, as she lifted it out of her purse and handed it to him. He placed it on his head and smiled with a nod of thanks.

After a minute, Patrick leaned toward Jeanette and whispered, "This is great. Thanks." Jeanette smiled and turned her head once again to look for David.

It was well into the second act when Donald's body was quietly removed from the dressing room and out the back door of the theater. Detective Hobbs made it clear to the director that no crew or cast member was to leave the theater once the performance was over. Detective Hobbs felt he had a captive collection of suspects since the only people allowed backstage were cast and crew. Security personnel were instructed to allow no one into the stage area and to let no one leave.

Jeanette became visibly upset when David had not returned. She had visions of his taking on this case all by himself and getting into a jam. She wouldn't put it past him to do so, but thought it odd that David did not return to tell her that he'd be going somewhere.

Mr. Landsberg went back to his office. Sergeant Asher was there waiting for him. Kent told her that no one was seated in row 'R,' seat 27. Sergeant Asher asked him to bring Mrs. Switzer to the office, even if it would be disruptive to the people. The manager wrote on a small piece of paper, "Mrs. Switzer, please come to the aisle immediately. This is an emergency. Thank you." He put "Seat 26" on the folded note and gave it to the first person in row 'R' who passed it along. Jeanette read it and felt the adrenaline shoot into her bloodstream believing that something had happened to David. Perhaps it had to do with the murder he thought he had heard through his amplification device.

Jeanette picked up her purse and in an embarrassed sort of way, excused herself as she moved toward the aisle. The people were very understanding as they figured that the note they passed along signaled an emergency.

When she got to the end of the row, Kent thanked her and said they had to go to his office.

"Is my husband okay?" Jeanette asked full of fear.

"We can't find him. He apparently called the police and then a detective called back asking me to find him."

"I hope nothing has happened to him."

"We've not heard of any problem, so I'm sure he is fine."

While Raoul and Renee were performing on stage, David did what all people who have ever been bound and gagged try to do, and that was to try to wiggle free. While he was a relatively strong man, there was very little give in the rope that bound his arms and legs, and being gagged, he couldn't shout. Unlike Indiana Jones, he was not able to fashion some heroic escape.

David glanced over to a table and saw Renee's head microphone. He remembered seeing her remove it and set it down before she tied his feet. He also recalled her saying something like "I don't speak in the next act, I'm not wearing this clumsy thing. I hate these things anyway."

With considerable effort, David was able to scoot an inch or two along the floor. So, he began inching toward the table where the microphone was resting.

Meanwhile in Kent's office, Jeanette told Sergeant Asher that David said he heard, or thought he heard, a murder backstage. She also said it was very unlike him not to tell her he'd be leaving. They were always very good about letting each other know of plans. Jeanette was certain David was in trouble and probably in danger.

Sergeant Asher thanked Jeanette for the information and told her she could return to the show if she wanted to. Jeanette didn't feel like returning to her seat so she remained in the manager's office hoping the police would soon have some good news.

While sitting and worrying, Jeanette remembered that Lou Searing, a detective and good friend of theirs was visiting friends in Haslett, a town adjacent to East Lansing where the Wharton Center is located. *Surely Lou would come over and help* thought Jeanette. *He, like David, is a member of Self Help for Hard of Hearing People and understands the frustrations of hearing loss.* Jeanette immediately went to the phone and called him.

Within twenty minutes Lou arrived and got briefed on what had taken place. He talked to Mr. Landsberg as well. Lou quickly concluded that David really did hear a murder and was now being held captive against his will. He asked Jeanette to check and see if their car was where they parked it. She left the theater with two ushers and was back in about five minutes to report that it was still there.

Sergeant Asher, who had been on the phone when Lou arrived, agreed with Lou that David was in the theater and most likely was backstage. Sergeant Asher then contacted Detective Hobbs,

"Detective Hobbs?"

"Yes."

"This is Detective Asher. What is your location?"

"I'm backstage at the Wharton Center. Are you in the theater?"

"Yes, I'm in the manager's office. We have a new situation developing. By the way, do you mind if I put you on a speaker phone?"

"No, that's fine."

"Here's what happening out here. A gentleman named David Switzer thought he heard a murder on his assistive listening device just before the play started. At intermission he told his wife he was going to let someone know what he'd heard. He called the police and I spoke with him. Our conversation was cut off and Mr. Switzer has not been seen since. Mrs. Switzer has been questioned and fears for her husband's safety. She called Lou Searing—you remember him. He's a private investigator that we've worked with. Lou and the Switzers are good friends."

"Yeah, I know Lou. He's a good guy. Is he there?"

"Yes, and he agrees that David is probably a hostage. They must've realized that someone overhead their crime and found out who it was."

"That's logical."

"What's happening backstage?" Detective Asher asked.

"We haven't had anybody come back here since I arrived."

"David could have been brought backstage during the intermission," Sergeant Asher suggested.

"That's possible but unlikely. Security is not letting anyone in or out. I doubt he's back here, but he could be, there are a lot of rooms and storage areas."

"Are you in agreement that the killer or killers are probably still in the theater and more than likely linked to the show?"

"Yes, I feel quite certain that whoever did it is either in the cast or a member of the crew. We're waiting for the performance to end before we begin questioning everyone."

"Everyone is to be kept backstage following the performance, I take it," Sergeant Asher confirmed.

"Yes, no one will leave and no one will get in. We've a lot of questions to ask and we'll need to identify everyone backstage when the murder took place and find out how to contact them once I release them."

"Got any advice for how we can help you?" Lou asked.

"I suppose there is the possibility of escape at curtain call. If you see any member of the cast take a bow and go into the audience instead of staying behind the curtain as it closes, track the person so we can apprehend the suspect."

"Will do. I think the show is due to be over in about 15 minutes or so."

"Correct."

In the laundry room David continued to inch toward the table holding the head microphone. All of his gyrating around caused the ropes to loosen a bit to where he thought he just might be able to eventually free himself. While trying to get his hands and feet free, he was also moving his jaw and mouth and using his teeth to pull a bit so that eventually the sash around his mouth loosened and fell onto his chest.

Meanwhile, Patrick seemed to be having trouble hearing the actors on stage because of a sound that he couldn't identify. It was a scraping sound and almost led to his taking off the headset. However, the amplified signal was helpful and gave him a much better listening edge even with the uncomfortable scraping sound.

It occurred to David that he may not need to get close to the microphone to be heard. He knew the headset was in Jeanette's purse and no one would hear it anyway, but he thought it worth an effort to get someone's attention. He also knew that others may have checked out a device and would be able to hear him.

"Jeanette! Jeanette! Help! I'm in the laundry room backstage."

Patrick noticed the strange voice but it didn't dominate his listening as he was concentrating on the play especially during the exciting moments of the second act.

David repeated his plea, "Jeanette!! Jeanette! HELP!" This time Patrick caught a bit of the message, if only that the voice was from someone in trouble.

Again David spoke. "I'm going to be murdered. Please help me!"

Patrick's wife could tell that something was bothering her husband.

"What's the matter?" she whispered.

"Shhh, I hear a murder," Patrick whispered so as not to disturb others around him.

"A what?"

"I think I hear a murder."

"It's in your imagination, Patrick. Shhh, watch the show," his wife said quietly shaking her head in disbelief.

Patrick directed his attention to the final scene of *Dr. Jekyll and Mr. Hyde* thinking that what he was hearing was in his imagination.

. . . .

David was almost free of the rope around his wrists and once free he'd be able to escape except he had a brilliant idea. He would put on one of the costumes and try to be inconspicuous in the backstage area so he wouldn't be discovered by the killers. He quickly threw the ropes away and found a costume of a 19th century Englishman. He thought this would be appropriate for *Dr. Jekyll and Mr. Hyde* and to his amazement it fit reasonably well. David found a rather large hat with a wide brim that he figured would help disguise his presence backstage.

Once in costume he took Renee's stage microphone and attached it to his head. He would continue to try and reach Jeanette.

David was lucky that the laundry room door could open from inside, but would lock to anyone on the outside. He decided to hide as best he could so he'd fit in behind the darkened set.

David didn't know the police were backstage investigating the murder and it was quite dark so he couldn't see them. His plan was to walk out on the stage with the cast for the bow and then as the curtain closed he would step in front of the curtain, shed the costume and quickly melt into the crowd exiting the theater. He found a spot to hide in between the set and a backstage curtain. He couldn't be seen and if he talked quietly into the microphone, nobody would hear him.

Patrick continued to use the device to listen to the production of *Dr. Jekyll and Mr. Hyde*. Unlike David, Patrick didn't feel embarrassed to excuse himself and go past twenty-five people. He had to report this new development. He got to the aisle and walked out into the lobby in search of the woman who gave him the headset, or the manager of the theater, or, if he were really lucky, a police officer. When Patrick got to the lobby he looked at the monitor with the live show. He saw something different, probably because he was not looking at the main characters but seemed to glance at two characters on stage who were talking to one another. This wasn't a logical part of the production. Patrick quickly matched the drama on his headset to these two actors on stage.

Patrick continued his search for someone who might make sense of the auditory and visual clues. He spotted Lou Searing standing in a doorway at the back of the theater. He knew Lou was a local writer and investigator because he had seen him in a number of newspaper articles and at a book signing or two. "Excuse me, Mr. Searing?"

"Yes, I'm Lou Searing."

"Boy, am I glad to see you. When I wear these headphones I hear someone in trouble and I noticed two actors, actually an actor and an actress, communicating about something on stage."

"Let me listen," Lou said.

Patrick gave Lou the headphones and as Lou placed them over his ears he heard David talking to himself or maybe talking to a ghost who he hoped was listening. Lou heard, "This is Dave Switzer. I'm backstage. A murder has been committed. Two people are responsible. If anyone is hearing this, please call the police." In a voice above a whisper, David kept repeating this except when an occasional crew member would walk by.

This message was sprinkled in with the actors' voices on stage so it wasn't perfectly clear to Lou, who had a hearing loss of his own, but he got enough of it to know that David was backstage, which confirmed his hunch.

Lou thanked Patrick for his timely appearance in the lobby and immediately called Detective Hobbs to report this development.

While this drama was going on, Raoul and Renee, the cast members responsible for the murder and for holding David captive, left the stage and returned to the laundry room.

When Detective Hobbs got to the laundry room he discovered two people obviously upset to discover David missing. Of course, the police detective thought he was coming upon someone held captive and not the murderers.

"Do you folks need my help?" the detective asked.

"No, just in here for a fresh shirt for the final scene, officer."

"Ok, just checking." The officer saw the rope and a suit coat on the floor. He became suspicious.

"Who are you folks? Identify yourselves."

"I'm Raoul and this is Renee. We've got to get back on stage. Key scene coming up in 15 seconds." The two literally ran out of the laundry room and headed to the left stage entrance.

David could tell the two of them were within a few feet of him and ready to make their entrance for the final scene. On cue, the two entered the stage and within seconds the play was over, the curtain closed and the cast quickly got into position for the curtain call.

Lou was positioned in the back of the theater to do as Detective Hobbs had asked—to track anyone who might escape from the front of the stage. Once again not realizing if he was being heard or not said, "The two who held me captive and who murdered the guy backstage are taking their bow at this moment. They're the fifth and sixth persons to the left of the actor who played the lead role." Lou clearly heard this message, took his cell phone and immediately called the manager to ask that the television recording of the production being shown in the lobby be kept on tape.

The audience was now giving the cast a standing ovation and the sound of the applause was deafening. David slipped onto the stage, joined in the bow with the intent of simply walking to freedom as the curtain closed. That would have worked well, except when he began to walk forward he couldn't. A stagehand had him in a bear hug and pulled him back. If anyone had seen what happened, he would think that it was an expression of joy, sort of a joyful hug to celebrate a great show coming to an end.

During this commotion, Raoul and Renee stepped in front of the closing curtain. They did not run out of the theater, but simply walked to the front of the stage to bend over and shake hands with people standing in the first row. They were smiling and jovial and the people were pleased to be able to shake hands with a Broadway actor and actress. However, the two did not return to the stage. They nonchalantly walked into the crowd of people to receive congratulations for a great show. Lou watched the two very carefully.

David was held against the floor backstage and this

brought lots of commotion. Most of the cast believed that he was an intruder since no one recognized him as a cast or crew member. By now the rumor of murder in the dressing room had gone throughout the cast and everyone thought the stagehand had captured the murderer. The police quickly appeared and took control, but the police didn't know what David looked like and for all they knew, David was indeed, the murderer.

David tried to explain that he had been held captive by two members of the cast, but everyone saw this as an excuse to try and explain why he'd be backstage.

Meanwhile, Lou was approached by two former neighbors who saw him and wanted to introduce him to their friends. Lou tried to be polite while glancing toward Raoul and Renee who were now getting more difficult to follow as they meshed in with the crowd exiting the theater. This distraction of a few seconds removed Lou's attention from the tracking. Lou graciously greeted the people and explained that he really must be on his way and he'd explain later. When he looked into the crowd, he could not see the two actors.

Patrick was standing in the lobby watching people and feeling rather useless. He glanced right and then left and there into his field of vision came the two actors he had seen on stage. He took a pen from his pocket and with his playbill in hand, he approached the two. "Marvelous performance. You two were phenomenal. Could I have your autographs? Please sign this to Noah who is an aspiring actor in high school. Write something like 'To Noah, Best wishes for a career in theater. May you reach the heights of success as I have.' Oh, and please sign it so he can clearly read your name. So many celebrities just scribble something and I want Noah to cherish this message for years to come. Would you do that for me?"

Raoul and Renee acknowledged his request but seemed to want to be on their way. "Listen, we'd like to do this, but we really must be getting backstage. We trust you under-stand?"

"Oh, please," Patrick pleaded. "You have no idea how much this would mean to Noah." He handed the program to Raoul and then to Renee. They didn't write all he requested but they did autograph the playbill to Noah, smiled and left.

Patrick knew he at least had a good set of fingerprints from both and a writing sample. If they were in fact criminals and if they escaped, he could provide the police with some good evidence.

Backstage, the police had restored order and had taken David off to a prop storage room. They didn't go into the dressing or the laundry rooms which were being treated as crime scenes. David tried to explain what had happened to him. Once Detective Hobbs realized who he was, he quickly set the others right. The detective was able to determine who had held David captive and also quickly realized that they were not backstage and had somehow gotten away.

As fate would have it, Raoul and Renee walked right into Lou Searing, literally, excusing themselves for bumping into him as they made their way to the exit with hundreds of theatergoers. Lou took his cell phone, explained his location and the two were apprehended and arrested a minute later outside the Wharton Center.

Epilogue

The forensic technicians were successful in obtaining all the crime scene information necessary to provide a tight case for the prosecutor. The trial followed in a few weeks and Raoul and Renee were convicted of murdering Donald and kidnapping David. Oh, the motive? Donald had borrowed a significant sum of money from the two actors and had informed them earlier in the day that he had no intention of re-paying the loan of almost $50,000.00.

The End

THE SEARING MYSTERIES

A Parting Thought

I hope you enjoyed my stories. Hearing loss is a frustrating experience. After living 57 years with these imperfect ears, I've learned that life is enhanced when I can smile at those experiences that give me opportunities to see the humor in a misunderstanding, temporary confusion, or my sometimes feeble attempts to make sense of the sound and communication going on around me. I urge you to smile at those circumstances that provide you with opportunities to see the humor in your interactions with others.

Thanks for reading. Follow your dreams. It's a great life!

Richard L. Baldwin

THE SEARING MYSTERIES

LISTEN TO THIS GREAT
FUNDRAISING OPPORTUNITY

Contact Buttonwood Press for information about fundraising opportunities for your organization. Selling **The Searing Mysteries** is a good way to share some fun stories and to support your organization. The plan is simple. Each book retails for $6.95, but you can save by bulk buying. Simply choose the number of books you plan to sell from the list below and fill in the order form that follows.

- 2-10 books = $4.95/book

    (Your profit margin is $2.00 for each book sold)

- 11-30 books = $4.45/book

    (Your profit margin is $2.50 for each book sold)

- 31+ books = $3.95/book

    (Your profit margin is $3.00 for each book sold)

I would like to order _____ copies of **The Searing Mysteries** at $_____ per copy. Enclosed is a check for $_____

Please ship to:

Name_____

Organization_____

Address_____

City/State/ZIP_____

Would you like Rich to autograph? ☐ Yes   ☐ No

Mail Order Form with a Check payable to:

Buttonwood Press
PO Box 716
Haslett, MI 48840

Fax: 517-339-5908
Email: RLBald@aol.com
Website: www.buttonwoodpress.com

Buttonwood Press will pay any applicable taxes as well as shipping and handling to further support your organization's fundraising efforts.

Questions? Email RLBald@aol.com or Fax Rich at 517-339-5908
Thank you!

BUTTONWOOD PRESS ORDER FORM

To order Richard Baldwin's Lou Searing and Margaret McMillan Mystery Series, four Michigan-based murder mysteries, visit the website of Buttonwood Press at www.buttonwoodpress.com for information or fill out the order form here. Thank you.

Name_____

Address_____

City/State/Zip_____

Book Title	Qty	Price
The Lou Searing and Magaret McMillan Mystery Series:		
A Lesson Plan for Murder ($12.95 – Softcover)		
The Principal Cause of Death ($12.95 – Softcover)		
Administration Can Be Murder ($12.95 – Softcover)		
Buried Secrets of Bois Blanc: Murder in the Straits of Mackinaw ($12.95 – Softcover)		
The Searing Mysteries – 3 Stories in 1 ($6.95 – Softcover)		
TOTAL		

Rich Baldwin will personally autograph a copy of any of his books for you. It's also a great gift for that mystery lover you know!

Autograph Request To:

_____

_____

_____

Mail Order Form with a Check payable to:

Buttonwood Press
PO Box 716
Haslett, MI 48840

Fax: 517-339-5908
Email: RLBald@aol.com
Website: www.buttonwoodpress.com

Questions? Call the Buttonwood Press office at (517) 339-9871
Thank you!